W9-CEO-540

READING RECOVERY

A Note to Parents

Rhyme, Repetition, and Reading are 3 R's that make learning fun for your child. **Rhyme Time Readers** will introduce your child to the sounds of language, providing the foundation for reading success.

Rhyme

Children learn to listen and to speak before they learn to read. When you read this book, you are helping your child connect spoken language to written language. This increased awareness of sound helps your child with phonics and other important reading skills. While reading this book, encourage your child to identify the rhyming words on each page.

Repetition

Rhyme Time Readers have stories that your child will ask you to read over and over again. The words will become memorable due to frequent readings. To keep it fresh, take turns reading, and encourage your child to chime in on the rhyming words.

Reading

Someday your child will be reading this book to you, as learning sounds leads to reading words and finally to reading stories like this one. I hope this book makes reading together a special experience.

Have fun and take the time
to let your child read and rhyme.

Francie Alexander

—Chief Education Officer,
Scholastic's Learning Ventures

To Margaret Gabel—with many thanks
—E.F.

For Hayden, Molly, and Griffin
—C.D.

ISBN: 0-439-33401-2

Text copyright © 2002 by Estelle Feldman.
Illustrations copyright © 2002 by Chris Demarest.
All rights reserved. Published by Scholastic Inc.
SCHOLASTIC, RHYME TIME READERS, CARTWHEEL BOOKS,
and associated logos are trademarks and/or registered trademarks of Scholastic Inc.

Library of Congress Cataloging-in-Publication Data

Feldman, Estelle, 1931-
    Snowy winter day / by Estelle Feldman ; illustrated by Chris Demarest.
       p.   cm.— (Rhyme time readers)
    Summary: Rhyming text describes some of the ways to play outside on a snowy day.
    ISBN 0-439-33401-2
    [1. Snow—Fiction. 2. Stories in rhyme.]   I. Demarest, Chris L., ill. II. Title.
III. Series.
PZ8.3.F3255 Sn 2002
[E]—dc21
    2001041129
    CIP
    AC

10 9 8 7 6 5 4 3   02 03 04 05 06

Printed in the U.S.A.
First printing, January 2002

· RHYME · TIME · READERS ·

Snowy Winter Day

by Estelle Feldman

Illustrated by Chris Demarest

SCHOLASTIC INC.
Cartwheel
·B·O·O·K·S·®

New York   Toronto   London   Auckland   Sydney
Mexico City   New Delhi   Hong Kong   Buenos Aires

On a snowy winter day ...
Build a snowman big and fat.

Carrot nose and tall black hat!

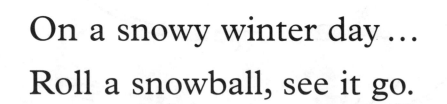

On a snowy winter day ...
Roll a snowball, see it go.

Watch it grow and grow
and grow.

On a snowy winter day…
Snowball fights are always fun.

Duck down quick—
here comes one!

On a snowy winter day ...
Pull a sled high up a hill.

Hold on tight, or ...
Tumble! Spill!

On a snowy winter day ...
Tramp the snow
deep on the ground.

Making tracks
as you go round.

On a snowy winter day…
Icy places make you slide.

Lace up your skates,
push off ... glide!

On a snowy winter day …
Make snow angels!
Spread arms wide …

Until Mom calls you inside.
Some more snow falls,
soft and deep,
at night when you are asleep.

Morning comes.

Run out and play!

One more snowy winter day!